A NOTE TO PARENTS

When your children are ready to "step into reading," giving them the right books—and lots of them—is as crucial as giving them the right food to eat. **Step into Reading Books** present exciting stories and information reinforced with lively, colorful illustrations that make learning to read fun, satisfying, and worthwhile. They are priced so that acquiring an entire library of them is affordable. And they are beginning readers with an important difference— they're written on four levels.

Step 1 Books, with their very large type and extremely simple vocabulary, have been created for the very youngest readers. **Step 2 Books** are both longer and slightly more difficult. **Step 3 Books,** written to mid-second-grade reading levels, are for the child who has acquired even greater reading skills. **Step 4 Books** offer exciting nonfiction for the increasingly proficient reader.

Copyright © by William Heinemann Ltd. 1993. All rights reserved under International and
Pan-American Copyright Conventions. Published in the United States by Random House, Inc.,
New York. All publishing rights: William Heinemann Ltd., London. All television and merchandising rights
licensed by William Heinemann Ltd. to Britt Allcroft (Thomas) Ltd. exclusively, worldwide.

Library of Congress Cataloging-in-Publication Data
Thomas and the school trip / illustrated by Owain Bell.   p.   cm.—
(Step into reading. A Step 1 book)   "Based on The railway series by the Rev. W. Awdry."
SUMMARY: Attempting to hurry through his work so that he can give some schoolchildren a ride, Thomas
the Tank Engine must overcome a series of obstacles.
ISBN 0-679-84365-5 (pbk.)—ISBN 0-679-94365-X (lib. bdg.)
[1. Railroads—Trains—Fiction.   2. School field trips—Fiction.]   I. Bell, Owain, ill.
II. Awdry, W. Railway series.   III. Series: Step into reading. Step 1 book.
PZ7.T3696 1993   [E]—dc20 92-33711

Manufactured in the United States of America   10 9 8 7 6 5 4 3

STEP INTO READING is a trademark of Random House, Inc.

Random House, Inc.   New York, Toronto, London, Sydney, Auckland

Step into Reading

THOMAS
and the
SCHOOL TRIP

Based on *The Railway Series*
by the Rev. W. Awdry

Illustrated by Owain Bell

A Step 1 Book

Random House 🏠 New York

It is a big day
in the train yard.
"Let's get ready!"
says Thomas
the Tank Engine.

Swish, swish.

The train yard is ready.

Rub, rub.

Scrub, scrub.

The engines are bright
and shiny.

Blue, green, red.

Thomas, Henry, and
James are ready too.

Even Sir Topham Hatt is ready.

Ready for what?
Children—
on a school trip!
"Peep! Peep!
Here they come!"
shouts Thomas.

"Hello, hello,"
he puffs.
"My name is Thomas.
Watch me push!
Watch me pull!"

Thomas has lots of fun.

But soon Thomas
has to go.
He has work to do
on his branch line.

Poor Thomas.

He is sad.

He wants to stay.

He wants to play.

Sir Topham Hatt
has an idea.
"Do your job, Thomas.
Then hurry back.
You can take
the children home.

"But remember.
You cannot be late.
You must be on time.
Or somebody else
will take the children."

"I will hurry.

I will hurry,"

Thomas says.

His coaches Annie

and Clarabel say,

"We will hurry too."

Chug, chug, chug.
All along his branch line,
Thomas goes as fast
as he can.

Up a hill.
Over a bridge.
Through a tunnel.
Thomas stops
at every station.

At last!

The work is done.

"Right on time.

Right on time,"

chugs Thomas.

"Now hurry back.

Hurry back,"

puff Annie and Clarabel.

But Thomas
cannot hurry.
Thomas has to wait.

And wait.

And wait again.

Oh no!

Will Thomas be late?

Will James or Henry

take the children home?

Oh my!
Now what is that
up ahead?
It is Bertie the Bus.
He has broken down.

Thomas wants to help.

But then he will be late—

much too late.

Stop or go.

Help or hurry.

What should Thomas do?

Screech!
Thomas stops.
He cannot leave
his friend.

"Will you take
my passengers?"
asks Bertie.

Look!

It is the children!

Bertie was taking

them home.

Hooray for Thomas!

He has saved the day!